SpongeBob SQUAREPANTS

The Great Train Mystery

adapted by David Lewman
based on the screenplay "Krabby Patty No More" written by Casey
Alexander, Zeus Cervas, Steven Banks & Dani Michaeli
illustrated by The Artifact Group

Ready-to-Read

Simon Spotlight/Nickelodeon
New York   London   Toronto   Sydney

Stephen Hillenburg

Based on the TV series *SpongeBob SquarePants*™ created by Stephen Hillenburg
as seen on Nickelodeon™

SIMON SPOTLIGHT/NICKELODEON
An imprint of Simon & Schuster Children's Publishing Division
1230 Avenue of the Americas, New York, New York 10020
For information about special discounts for bulk purchases, please contact Simon & Schuster Special Sales at 1-866-506-1949 or
business@simonandschuster.com.
Manufactured in the United States of America 0711 LAK
6 8 10 9 7 5
ISBN 978-1-4424-0782-4

"SpongeBob!" yelled Mr. Krabs.
"I need you to cross the ocean and
  bring back the secret Krabby Patty
  recipe I keep hidden in Way Far-Out
  Townville."
"Yes, sir!" said SpongeBob.

Mr. Krabs held up a key. "This is the only key to the safe deposit box that has the recipe locked inside." He handed it to SpongeBob. "I will guard this key with my life," SpongeBob promised.

"ALL ABOARD!"

SpongeBob waved from the train.
"Good-bye, Mr. Krabs! Wish me luck!"

Mr. Krabs shouted, "Remember, boy,
keep your eye on that key!
And watch out for Plankton!"

"Thanks for coming with me, buddy,"
SpongeBob told Patrick. "Mr. Krabs
is counting on me to bring back
the Krabby Patty recipe!"
"Mmm, Krabby Patties," Patrick moaned.
His pal agreed. "To the dining car!"

Meanwhile, Plankton knew of SpongeBob's mission and wanted the key. "I'll hop on the train and steal the key because I am an EVIL GENIUS!" he shouted.

SpongeBob and Patrick walked
into the dining car.
"Ooh, fancy!" SpongeBob gushed.
"And they give you so much food,
you need two forks!" cried Patrick.

They heard a baby crying.
"I can't get the poor dear to stop!"
said its nanny.
"It's okay, little fella. No need
to fuss," SpongeBob said.

They sat down and a porter came in.

"Wow!" SpongeBob said.

"A real live butler!"

"I am NOT a butler," the porter said.

"Sorry, sir, but the dining car
    is closed!"

"But we haven't even heard the
specials yet," SpongeBob said.
"The dining car is closed for you!"
the porter growled. "You must
leave now!" He shoved
SpongeBob out of his seat.

"Hope next time we get to eat,"
said Patrick.

"We have to find a safe place to
hide this," SpongeBob said.

"Hide what?" asked Patrick.

"THE KEY!" SpongeBob screamed.
"Patrick, where's the key?
I promised Mr. Krabs
I would not let it out
of my sight!"

Suddenly SpongeBob and Patrick
noticed Plankton aboard the train.
"Plankton! YOU stole the key!"
SpongeBob shouted.
"Oh, come on!" Plankton said.
"I just got here! I couldn't have
stolen it . . . yet."

"Search him! SpongeBob said.
"With pleasure!" Patrick answered.
Patrick picked up Plankton.
He stared at the tiny guy.
"He's clean," Patrick said.
"I told you!" Plankton shouted.

"Well, if you did not steal it,
then who did?"
SpongeBob thought hard.
"It must have been someone
on this train! Patrick, call the cops!"

"COPS! I NEED YOU!" Patrick bellowed.

"A great mystery has taken place today," SpongeBob told the police officers. "Someone on board this train must have stolen the key."

Suddenly he pointed. "You there! You are not fooling me with that innocent act!"

"Where were you at six p.m.
the night of May fifth?
And don't you give me that
goo goo gaa gaa stuff!"

SpongeBob walked up to the police
chief. "I believe the thief is
none other than . . .
THE NANNY!"
The nanny laughed nervously.
"I have not stolen a key!"

SpongeBob picked up the baby.
"Sir, if you search this baby's
diaper, you will find the key!"
The police chief took out
a pair of tongs.
He started to search. . . .

"Aha!" cried the police chief.
SpongeBob was thrilled. "The key!"
"No," said the chief. "Neptune's
Jewel of the Sea! You've nabbed
the Jewel Triplets Gang!"

"Triplets?" asked SpongeBob.
"Yes, triplets," said the baby in
a rough, low voice. "Come on out,
you two. They got us."
The nanny opened her coat.
She was really two brothers!

SpongeBob was shocked.
"So, if they didn't do it,
that means the key was
stolen by . . ."

"The butler!" SpongeBob turned
and pointed at the porter.
Plankton jumped on the porter's
chest. "Give me the key!
Give it to me!" he roared.
SpongeBob told the biggest
police officer to shake
the butler down.

The policeman shook the porter.

First Plankton hit the ground.

Then a stapler hit Plankton. BONK!

Then a hammer. CLONK!

Then an anvil. CLANG!

"No key," the cop said. But then . . .

the porter's MASK slid off!

The cop was amazed!
"This is Oren J. Roughy!
He's wanted for stealing
ham sandwiches!"
Patrick shook his head.
"That's a TERRIBLE crime!"

But SpongeBob started to cry.
"I still have not found the key!
I broke my promise to Mr. Krabs!
I don't deserve to work
at the Krusty Krab!"

"Don't worry, buddy," Patrick said.
"I'm sure it will turn up." He was
cleaning his teeth with something.
And that something was . . .
THE KEY!

"Patrick!" SpongeBob yelled.
"Where in the ocean did you find
the key?"

"In your shorts," Patrick answered.
"When I was cleaning them from
your little 'accident' earlier."
SpongeBob blushed.

"Now the mystery is solved
and we can go get the recipe,"
SpongeBob said. "The key is
safe with me!"
"For now," Plankton said as he followed
them onto the train.